ENCHANTED PONY ACADEMY

Wings That Shine

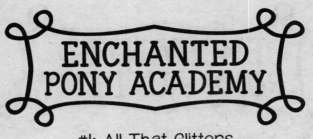

ENCHANTED PONY ACADEMY

ENCHANTED PONY ACADEMY

Wings That Shine

* Lisa Ann Scott *

* illustrated by Heather Burns *

SCHOLASTIC INC.

Text copyright © 2017 by Lisa Ann Scott

Illustrations by Heather Burns, © 2017 Scholastic Inc.

All rights reserved. Published by Scholastic Inc., *Publishers since 1920.* SCHOLASTIC and associated logos are trademarks and/or registered trademarks of Scholastic Inc.

The publisher does not have any control over and does not assume any responsibility for author or third-party websites or their content.

No part of this publication may be reproduced, stored in a retrieval system, or transmitted in any form or by any means, electronic, mechanical, photocopying, recording, or otherwise, without written permission of the publisher. For information regarding permission, write to Scholastic Inc., Attention: Permissions Department, 557 Broadway, New York, NY 10012.

This book is a work of fiction. Names, characters, places, and incidents are either the product of the author's imagination or are used fictitiously, and any resemblance to actual persons, living or dead, business establishments, events, or locales is entirely coincidental.

ISBN 978-0-545-90891-7

10 9 8 7 6 5 4 3 2 1   17 18 19 20 21

Printed in the U.S.A.   40

First printing 2017

Book design by Yaffa Jaskoll

To my son, Jack,
who is as strong and awesome
as Duke. Love you!

CHAPTER 1

Skydancer rustled her wings in excitement as she listened to plans for the Homecoming celebration. It was her first month at the Enchanted Pony Academy, the magical school hidden beyond the clouds. At the academy she and the other Glitter Ponies worked on their magic to become pets for the royal children of the hundred kingdoms.

"Homecoming is our first competition between the four barns," explained Belissima, the lead pony of Skydancer's barn, Earth barn. There were four barns at the school: Earth, Sun, Sky, and Water. "Homecoming is so much fun!"

Skydancer's best friend, Daisy, swished her tail and smiled. Every pony had a Glitter Gift, but Daisy had one of the most incredible ones. She could turn invisible! And she was a wonderful friend.

"We must have the best float for the school-spirit contest," Belissima went on, pacing up and down at the front of their barn. "We'll use our magical talents to create an amazing float and then enter it in the parade around the exhibition field. Earth barn almost always wins, but we need some great ideas. Anyone have something spec-tacular in mind?"

"I could put on a fireworks show," said Stone, stomping his hooves. His Glitter Gift was making sparks shoot from his horn and he loved playing tricks and surprising other ponies. "Turn my sparks into fireworks!" A few pops fizzled from his horn.

"Your spell didn't rhyme. Of course it didn't work!" said Lavender, making a row of posies bloom at her feet. She loved show-ing off her cool Glitter Gift. "I can certainly provide some flowers for the float!"

Skydancer swished her tail. "I will ask my bird friends if they can fly along with the float and sing." Since her Glitter Gift was talking to other winged creatures, she knew she could get them to help.

"Great! We have to work together to create something amazing," Belissima said. "But the student who works the hardest and contributes the most out of all the students in the four barns will be named Grand Pony Marshal of the Homecoming parade. The marshal even gets to pull the golden chariot

around the track, leading the floats! All our former students will be returning to the school with their royal children for the celebration! Your families can come, too. It's a wonderful day."

The ponies started whinnying and chattering.

"And you get to wear *this*." Belissima levitated a beautiful medal in front of the group. The rare gems from each barn were embedded in a gold circle. "This medal has been worn by the Grand Pony Marshal at Homecoming for hundreds of years. Usually, second-year ponies win that honor, but you never know! Maybe it'll be your turn next. Pass it around for a closer look at it. But be careful. It is very old and very precious."

The ponies took turns admiring the incredible piece. Skydancer could imagine it shining brightly on her chest as she pranced around the exhibition field. Her parents would be so proud! She was their only pony, and they expected big things from her. That medal would prove she was as special as they hoped she'd be. And wouldn't that be a great way to prove she'd be a perfect pet for the royal children someday? She was going to work her hardest on the float so she could be named Grand Pony Marshal.

"Let's get busy. Homecoming is in less than a week." Belissima took back the medal.

Skydancer couldn't wait to talk to her bird friends for some float ideas. Maybe she could lasso a cloud and make it look like the float was . . . floating? Skydancer chuckled, amused by the funny thought.

As the ponies started leaving, Belissima stopped Skydancer. "Could you fly this back to Headmaster Elegius? He wants to put it away for safekeeping. We're lucky he even let us look at it." She gave her the medal.

"No problem." Skydancer liked being helpful, especially here at the academy. Someday,

she'd be helping her future owner, one of the royal children of the hundred kingdoms. She and the other ponies had to practice being of service.

With the medal hanging around her neck, Skydancer flew toward the castle. The headmaster's office was in one of the tall turrets. Skydancer soared through the air feeling positively majestic.

I don't have to go straight to his office, do I? she wondered. *I'll take it back in a little while. I'm going to enjoy this a bit longer.*

She swooped through the air over the training fields, then above the apple orchards. She had to be careful not to leave school grounds. That wasn't allowed.

She flew over the river, wondering if she'd see one of the seaponies rising to the surface. Skydancer and her friends had ventured out to spy on them when they'd first arrived at school. Later, Daisy befriended a seapony named Marina, trading apples for their delicious seaweed that grew in great forests underwater. Marina loved hearing about the Enchanted Pony Academy and comparing it to the school the seaponies attended to become helpers for the royal mer-children.

Wouldn't Marina be impressed if Skydancer became Grand Pony Marshal? Her parents would be, too. *Everyone* would be impressed. She was only a first-year student.

She flapped her wings in the breeze, closing her eyes as she imagined the cheers she'd receive as Grand Pony Marshal.

"Skydancer! Skydancer!" everyone would chant. She could almost hear her name ringing out across the field.

She opened her eyes. She really could hear her name being called. Several bird friends were flying alongside her trying to get her attention.

"Skydancer!" a bird called. "Stop!"

CHAPTER 2

W hat's wrong?" Skydancer asked.

"You're too far away from the academy!" a sweet little red bird cried.

Skydancer slowed down and realized she was in the middle of a cloud. "Where am I?" she asked nervously. She didn't like being lost. And she definitely didn't like feeling scared.

"You're in the cloud bank right by the

craggy canyon!" a big black bird told her, angrily. "You're not supposed to be here! It's so far away from school!"

"We tried to warn you, but you weren't listening!" a blue bird said.

Flapping her wings, Skydancer hovered in the air. "Thanks for stopping me," she said to the birds. "I can't imagine going anywhere near the craggy canyon." The huge canyon surrounding the school helped keep it hidden so outsiders would stay away. She'd never seen it, but had heard it was incredibly scary, with jagged rocks jutting out and wild creatures filling it with their cries. The cloud bank formed a barrier between the canyon and the school as extra protection. Most ponies had never even seen the canyon.

Most ponies had never even come near the cloud bank.

"Hurry up and go back to school before you get in trouble!" the birds called as they flew away.

"I will! Thanks!" She hadn't even had time to ask them about helping with the float. But that was the least of her worries. Skydancer had no idea which way to go to get back to school. She flew straight ahead, but she was still in the cloud. She flew to the side and then in the other direction until she realized she was flying in circles! Would she be stuck in this cloud bank forever? She was terrified.

Frustrated, Skydancer sped straight forward, certain she was headed toward the castle. Her racing heart slowed as she saw the cloud disappearing ahead. She must be going in the right direction.

But then she heard shrieks and howls, and she knew she wasn't flying toward the castle. She was flying right above the craggy canyon!

She skidded to a halt in the air, terrified to fly too far over the deep gorge in the earth. But when she did, something awful happened. The medal flew off Skydancer's neck and tumbled into the canyon.

"Oh no!" She watched it fall into the deep abyss until it caught on a branch jutting out from the canyon wall. She could just barely see the bright glint of metal far below. Screeches and howls rose from the bottom of the pit.

Tears filled her eyes. She was going to be in so much trouble—if she could even find her way back home. For a moment, she thought about flying down into the canyon to get it. But she was much too scared. What if her wings caught on a branch? What if something reached out and grabbed her?

Skydancer hung her head. What child would want such a frightened pony for a pet? She was concentrating on guardianship in her studies. She would have to be brave to help the royal children rule their lands. How in the world could she ever learn to be more courageous?

She turned straight around and flew as fast as she could through the clouds, hoping she was headed toward the castle this time. Her heart stopped pounding so hard when she heard her bird friends calling for her. She really was headed in the right direction.

"Skydancer! Skydancer! Where are you?"

"I'm coming, I'm coming!" She flapped her wings, feeling exhausted.

"Hurry, we need your help!"

Skydancer flew toward their voices. Whatever could be the matter? She'd been the one in trouble—now they were, too?

Finally, she flew out of the cloud bank.

"There's something on the edge of the forest, just ahead!" cried the big black bird. "Something . . . scary."

"What is it?" Skydancer asked nervously.

"I'm not sure," said the red bird. "I think . . . I think it's a dragon."

CHAPTER 3

Stunned and tired, Skydancer landed on the ground. She laughed softly, certain the birds were joking.

"It's not a dragon. The dragons left years ago, during the Age of Recklessness."

Many, many years ago, careless spell casting had weakened the magic in the land, and most of the magical creatures had fled. According to legends, they still lived, but remained hidden in their own secret worlds.

But no one had seen a dragon in hundreds of years. There certainly wasn't one lurking in the forest by the school.

"Stop teasing me," Skydancer said.

"We're not!" the birds shrieked. Something had genuinely spooked them. Skydancer wasn't so sure she wanted to see what it was. She was good at many things, but being brave wasn't one of them.

"I'd better get back to the school," she said, wondering how she was ever going to find the courage to admit she'd lost the medal.

"No, you have to come and see it and then get help!" a bird called.

The birds *must* be mistaken. Whatever they were seeing couldn't be a dragon, Skydancer was sure. Still, she was frightened, frozen in place. "Where is it?" Why was she such a scaredy pony?

"Just ahead, come on."

"Well, okay, I guess. I'll just fly over it." That way, she could speed off if it truly was something terrifying.

Slowly, Skydancer took to the air on gentle wings. She soared above the trees with the birds.

"Up ahead, right there at the edge of the woods!" they called to her.

Skydancer spotted something dark lying on the ground. It wasn't that big. It wasn't moving, and it wasn't roaring or bellowing fire, so she flew lower for a better look.

As she got closer, dark-blue scales came into view, as well as a long, spiky tail wrapped tightly around the creature's body. Skydancer's heart started racing.

She heard the soft puffs of snoring and flew in front of the thing. Its wings were tucked tightly against its body, but she could see its ribs rising and falling with each breath. It had dull, ragged scales. It was a dragon! A baby dragon.

And just then, it opened its big yellowy-orange eyes.

Skydancer nickered in fright and flew off to the castle without looking back. Her heart raced and her teeth chattered; she was so scared.

As the school came into view, she noticed a crowd was gathered outside the main entrance to the castle. It was close to dinnertime, and ponies were probably headed to the banquet hall. She spotted Headmaster Elegius's tricorn immediately, with the three horns meeting at the tip—silver, gold, and iridescent—sparkling in the sun. He would know what to do.

She landed next to the group, struggling to get any words out of her mouth.

Headmaster Elegius looked concerned. "What's wrong, Skydancer?"

"Drag . . . Drag . . ."

"You don't seem to be dragging any-thing," her friend Electra said.

"Dragon," she finally managed to say. "I just saw a dragon on the edge of the forest!"

Everyone was silent for a moment. Then all the ponies laughed. "Dragons are long gone," Stone said. "What a joker you are."

All the ponies laughed even harder.

"Skydancer, we don't have time to fool around," Belissima said, stomping her hoof. "We have a lot of work to do on the float!"

"But I saw it! It was a baby dragon. Dark blue. It was sleeping. But it saw me."

"What color were its eyes?" Headmaster Elegius asked.

"A yellowy orange."

Headmaster Elegius shared a look with Headmistress Valincia. "We better investigate. You ponies stay here. Gather in the great hall and stay together. The lead ponies are in charge. I'll send out a message."

A shiny orb sailed into the air from his horn, and then it popped, releasing his message in a voice so loud, every pony across the campus could hear it. *"All students report to the great hall immediately. Teachers, join me at the main gates. This is not a drill."*

None of the other ponies was laughing now. They stood silently, eyes wide.

"Get to the great hall!" Headmaster Elegius commanded.

The ponies galloped into the building, which was soon filled with all the students and their worried whispers.

"What's going on?" Skydancer's friend Razzle asked.

"Skydancer says she saw a dragon. The teachers are going to investigate," Electra explained.

Daisy hurried over. "You really saw a dragon?"

Everyone was listening. "Yes. At the edge of the forest. It was a baby, sleeping on the ground. It looked sick."

"What were you doing over there?" Belissima asked.

Skydancer's heart dropped, remembering her other big problem. The medal, now lost forever. "I was out flying, thinking of ideas for the float, and I got distracted. I ended up lost in the cloud bank."

A few ponies gasped. "The cloud bank?" Electra asked.

"That's off school grounds," Daisy said.

"And it's near the craggy canyon," Duke said. He was an enormous allapony, with wings and a horn. He was strong and brave, and even he looked concerned.

Skydancer didn't reply.

"Did the dragon say anything to you?" Daisy asked.

Skydancer shook her head.

The ponies gathered by the front door,

looking out the big windows on either side of it. The teachers were headed toward the forest.

"I wonder what's going to happen?" Electra asked. "Why would a dragon come here?"

"I don't know," Belissima said, her beautiful voice sounding calm. "But don't worry.

The dragon is far from the academy, and the teachers will take care of it. Let's not spend one minute thinking about it. Why don't we use this time to break into groups and work on plans for Homecoming?"

The ponies followed her suggestion, but everyone was talking softly, glancing out the windows instead of working on Homecoming ideas. The teachers were now out of sight.

"I wonder how a baby got here by itself?" Daisy whispered to Skydancer.

She gulped. "That's a good question."

"There was just one, right?" Daisy asked.

Skydancer nodded. "Thank goodness. I can't imagine a baby dragon could do much harm." Then her ears pricked up.

"What is it?"

"I hear something." Skydancer ran to the other side of the room where windows faced the school courtyard. And there sat another dragon. A much bigger dragon, about twice the size of a pony, with dull-green scales and those big yellowy-orange eyes.

Staring right at Skydancer.

CHAPTER 4

Behind Skydancer, several ponies whinnied in fright.

"A dragon! Right here at school! What are we going to do?" Electra asked as she huddled in a group of other first-year ponies.

"We're going to head to the banquet hall," Belissima said.

"Line up by barns," said Ranger, the leader of the Water barn. "Follow your lead pony."

But no one moved. They were all staring out the window. Then they jumped as the dragon roared.

Skydancer gasped while the other ponies shrieked. It wasn't trying to scare them. "You guys, it's calling for help," she said.

"It's a dragon! They're dangerous," cried Rose.

The other ponies all started talking at once.

"What should we do?" Razzle asked.

"Nothing!" Stone said. "It's a trap! The dragon is trying to get us to go outside so it can attack us."

The dragon roared again, not so loudly this time. Then it slumped its head to the ground, its eyelids drooping.

"What did it say?" Belissima asked.

"Water," Skydancer said. "It needs water."
She backed away from the window as the
dragon softly whimpered.

"What should we do?" Daisy asked.

"Get to the banquet hall, like we said,"
Ranger said sharply.

"But the poor thing could die," Daisy whispered.

"And so could we!" Stone replied. "We can't risk helping it."

Skydancer took a deep breath and raised her head to peer into the creature's eyes. They were half closed and dull looking. Its chest was heaving, and she could see its ribs. It looked as sick as the baby she had seen.

"Guys, I don't think it's trying to trick us," Skydancer told the other ponies. "It really seems to be sick. We have to help it. Someone bring it some water."

"I'm not doing it," Stone said as the rest of the ponies backed away from the window.

"You go," shouted a pony at Skydancer.

"You're the one who can talk to flying animals."

Skydancer said nothing. Neither did anyone else. No one was brave enough to go out there.

"I'll help you," Daisy said quietly.

Despite her fast-beating heart, Skydancer nodded. She felt a little less scared knowing she wouldn't have to go out there alone.

"Thanks. You're such a good friend. Let's get some buckets of water."

All the ponies galloped down to the banquet hall.

"I don't know about this," Belissima said, running next to Skydancer and Daisy. "The headmaster might be mad at us for interacting with a dragon."

"Then he can be mad at me," Skydancer said, surprising herself. "I can't stand by and watch it suffer." Her words sounded brave, but she certainly didn't feel that way. She was frightened. But that didn't stop her from helping Daisy gather buckets in the banquet hall. Next, she stomped on the marble floor, charging up her magic so she could cast a spell. Glitter billowed from her sparkly hooves.

"Fill these buckets to the brink, so we may offer the dragon a drink," Skydancer said. Spells worked best when cast in a rhyme.

Water soon rose in the buckets, filling them to the brim.

Daisy helped Skydancer load the water onto a cart, and they pulled it back to the great hall. All the ponies followed them, too upset and curious to stay behind.

Skydancer stood in front of the door, gathering the courage to go outside. "Does anyone else want to come?"

No one answered. So she nudged the door open with her nose and pulled the wagon outside, but she didn't see Daisy following her. She felt disappointed. Daisy had promised to help. *Guess I'm going to have to do this by myself.*

Slowly, the dragon—a female, Skydancer realized—raised her head.

Skydancer was terrified being this close

to a dragon so big. She cleared her throat. "You said you were thirsty?"

The dragon's eyes widened. "You can understand me?"

Skydancer nodded. "It's my Glitter Gift. I can talk to other winged creatures."

"Can you bring the water here? I'm too weak to move."

Now Skydancer's heart was racing. She'd have to get awfully close to the dragon to do that. Was it a trap like Stone had suggested?

Then suddenly the cart started moving on its own, traveling right over to the dragon. The dragon grabbed a bucket with her long, sharp teeth and drained it.

Skydancer heard the patter of hooves headed her way, and Daisy appeared. Daisy was the only pony whose hooves didn't make glitter. But that was a blessing, since her Glitter Gift was the ability to turn invisible. A trail of glitter would give her away.

"I didn't know you came with me!" Skydancer said.

"One of the perks of my gift." Daisy smiled.

After finishing all four buckets, the dragon sat up. "Thank you," she said. "I'm feeling a bit better. I'm Emerline."

"I'm Skydancer, and this is Daisy. What are you doing here?"

"Looking for food. I brought my little brother, Azule, with me. Our food supply has run out. We were the only ones strong enough to come looking for help. But he was too weak to even reach the school."

Skydancer felt a lump forming in her throat. Dragons ate meat, didn't they? Did the pony academy seem like a great big banquet? And here she and her best friend were standing right in front of one, waiting to be eaten!

"What kind of food are you looking for?" Skydancer did her best to sound calm.

"Fruits. Vegetables," Emerline replied. "We stopped eating meat long ago, when the animals died out. Now we just eat vegetation. But we haven't had rain in months. Nothing is growing. We'll eat anything. We certainly don't have the strength to fly back home." The dragon lowered her head.

Skydancer had no idea what to do. How

could she possibly help? "Let me ask the others for some ideas."

Skydancer and Daisy galloped back inside and explained everything.

"She said they'd eat anything," Skydancer said.

"Right, like us!" Stone said. "That's what it really wants. Tell it to go away."

"We shouldn't be helping it without talking to the teachers," Razzle said.

"But what if she dies from hunger?" Daisy asked. "That would be awful."

"It's not our problem," Stone huffed.

"Tell her to go somewhere else," another pony called out.

Anger was taking the place of fear in Skydancer's heart.

"There is a creature here begging for help," she said loudly. "I'm certain the teachers will understand. If not, I'm willing to take the risk. If anyone else wants to help me gather some food, follow me to the banquet hall."

"You're going to be sorry," Stone insisted. "You can't trust dragons."

"We'll see."

Skydancer hurried back down the hall, desperately hoping he was wrong.

CHAPTER 5

The ponies from Earth barn helped Skydancer load carrots and apples onto a cart. Skydancer pulled it outside and left it near the dragon.

Emerline quickly ate everything and was able to stretch out. The enormous talons on her feet scraped the dirt as she moved. "I need to get some food to my brother."

"The teachers went to see him," Skydancer told her.

"Can any of them talk to dragons?"

"No." Skydancer frowned.

"Please come with me to help him."

Skydancer backed away from Emerline. She couldn't stop thinking about Stone's warning, that dragons couldn't be trusted. She couldn't imagine what the teachers would say if she showed up with a dragon when the ponies had been told to stay at the school.

"I don't think I can."

"Please. They won't know what he needs. He's starving. We have nowhere else to go."

No one else could speak to dragons. And Emerline looked so sad. But Skydancer was scared. Could two dragons overtake a whole pack of ponies?

"Is there at least more food that I could bring him?" Emerline asked.

"We have apples in the orchard," Skydancer suggested. "Let me talk to the lead pony."

Skydancer went inside and explained the situation.

"The headmaster insisted we stay here," Belissima said. "I forbid you to leave."

Skydancer felt like backing into a corner, or running to her stall to be alone. But she couldn't stop thinking about that baby dragon who had looked so sick. What if he died? If she didn't help them, who would? She raised her head.

"They need me, Belissima. If I get in trouble, that's fine. I'll face the consequences, but it'll be worth it knowing I helped."

Then Skydancer turned and galloped out into the courtyard before anyone could stop her. "I'll come with you," she told Emerline. "We'll get apples on the way."

"Oh, thank you so much," the dragon said.

Skydancer clamped her teeth onto a bushel basket so she could collect some apples, then lifted off the ground. Slowly, the dragon followed her, Emerline's wings creating an immense shadow on the ground and a strong breeze in the air.

Skydancer flew in the direction of the spot where she had seen the baby dragon. She was going to be in so much trouble for disobeying the headmaster's orders. And for losing the medal! She'd forgotten all about that. Which problem was bigger: the dragons or the medal? She wasn't sure. No way would she be Grand Pony Marshal for the parade. Maybe she'd even get kicked out of school for everything she'd done.

She blinked back tears. She couldn't worry about that now. She had to help baby Azule before it was too late.

Skydancer landed in the apple orchard and quickly filled the bushel basket, while Emerline gorged on fallen fruit.

Tears streamed down the dragon's scaly cheeks. "I haven't had this much food in months."

Skydancer couldn't imagine what it felt like to be that hungry. "I'm sorry it's been so hard for you."

"Everyone back home is counting on me

to fix our food problems. I can't let them down. I was so scared to come here, but I didn't know what else to do."

Skydancer was shocked. Emerline was a good-size dragon, and she was scared? "Don't worry. Everything will be fine," she told the dragon. But she wasn't sure she believed it.

Once the basket was full of apples, they took off into the air again. Skydancer spotted the teachers standing in a circle around Emerline's baby brother.

The teachers looked up as Skydancer and Emerline landed.

"Another dragon?" Headmistress Valincia asked, backing up, her eyes wide. "How many are here?"

"Just these two. She landed in the court-yard after you left," Skydancer explained. "We didn't know what to do."

"Why aren't you back with the other students?" Headmaster Elegius demanded. "I ordered you all to stay put at school."

Skydancer's legs felt shaky, like she might topple to the ground. She had never heard the headmaster talk angrily to a student before.

"Why did you disobey my command?"

Skydancer was so scared. Could she get kicked out of school for this? But what else could she have done? The dragons were in trouble, and she had the power to help them.

"I . . . I'm pretty sure I'm the only one in the school who can talk to dragons."

"That's true," Headmistress Valincia said.

"So I thought I could help everyone understand what's going on."

The teachers nodded.

"You're right. Your Glitter Gift will be most helpful," Headmaster Elegius said, not sounding quite so angry. "Please, tell us what you know. Why are the dragons here? What do they want?"

"This is Emerline, and that's her little brother, Azule. There's no food left in their world. They eat vegetation now, and there's a drought in their land. They were the only two strong enough to come look for help. These apples are for Azule." Skydancer dragged the bushel of apples over to the sickly little dragon.

He opened one eye and tried to reach for the apples with his scaly paw, but couldn't. Skydancer tipped the basket over so the apples tumbled out. She rolled one toward Azule's mouth, and he closed his lips around it.

"He needs water, too." Skydancer helped

the little dragon eat a few more apples while two teachers left to get water.

The creature's eyes slowly opened wider as he filled his belly with food. "Thank you," he whispered.

Skydancer felt her eyes brimming with tears. The poor thing looked so sick. "You're welcome."

"Once we've fed them and given them a place to sleep for the night, I think they should be on their way," Professor Xayide said. "This doesn't feel safe."

"Are you leaving soon?" Skydancer asked Emerline.

"After we're rested and feeling stronger. We thank you for the food, but we have an even bigger favor to ask."

"What?" Skydancer asked.

"We need ponies to come back to our land with us."

CHAPTER 6

Headmaster Elegius gasped when Skydancer told him what the dragons wanted. "Impossible! Dragons and ponies have never been friendly."

"That was hundreds of years ago!" Skydancer was surprised she was arguing with a teacher, but she couldn't stop herself. "They need our help!"

"What do they think we can do for them?" Headmistress Valincia asked.

Skydancer turned to Emerline. "How can we help you?"

"We need your magic to help our crops grow faster," the dragon explained. "We need your magic to make it rain."

Skydancer shared their request with the teachers.

Headmaster Elegius paused for a few moments. "How far away is their land?"

Skydancer asked the weary dragon. "Headmaster, they're three days from here. Could you teleport there?"

Elegius shook his head. "That is too far for teleporting."

"One thing's for sure," tiny Professor Xayide said, zipping through the air as he spoke. "They can't stay here for long. Not

while our former students return with their owners for Homecoming. Imagine the panic if humans knew dragons had returned."

The rest of the teachers nodded in agreement.

"It's getting late. Let's go back to the school and discuss our options. The dragons can stay in the courtyard so we can keep an eye on them," Headmistress Valincia said, her pure silver coat and horn glinting in the setting sun. "Skydancer, tell the dragons we'll have a decision in the morning on whether we can assist them."

Skydancer explained everything to Azule and Emerline as they flew back to the castle.

"We thank you," Emerline said. "Without

your help, the dragons will die. We will be gone from this world."

The dragons settled into the courtyard for the night with the teachers swapping turns watching over them.

The ponies in the Earth barn couldn't sleep. "I never thought I'd see a dragon," Belissima said. "They're frightening to look at."

"They smell weird," said Razzle, wrinkling her nose.

"I don't think I'll be able to sleep until they leave," Lavender said.

Skydancer felt sad to hear how the other ponies were talking about the dragons. "They haven't hurt us. They just need our help."

"I'll just feel better when they're gone," said Razzle.

"Me too. We lost a whole day's work on the Homecoming float. We've got to work really hard tomorrow, so spend some time tonight thinking about your plans," Belissima said. "I'm going to be so disappointed if Earth barn doesn't win."

Chattering about their plans, the ponies went to their stalls. Even the beautiful scenes of meadows and fields in her room couldn't cheer up Skydancer.

"Goodnight," said Daisy, who shared the stall with her. "I'm exhausted after this day." She snuggled down in her bed of hay and quickly fell asleep.

But Skydancer couldn't stop replaying all the events in her head: the lost medal, the fear that had rippled through her when she first spotted the dragons. The concern about what would happen to them now. It certainly seemed as though there were nothing more she could do to help. She didn't even have time to worry about the

Homecoming float—or the lost medal. She groaned. Belissima would be so disappointed in her. Her parents, too. But she was more concerned about those poor, poor dragons. What could she do? She was just a young pony, and a scared one at that. She couldn't be of any help at all.

CHAPTER 7

The next morning on the way to breakfast, Skydancer saw the dragons munching huge piles of carrots in the courtyard.

"I hope they don't eat all our food," Razzle said.

"Are they leaving today? I feel so nervous with them here," said Violet, a unipony from Sky barn.

How are the dragons going to grow food

again in their land? Skydancer wondered. The teachers had to have a plan.

Skydancer was enjoying some oats in the banquet hall when Headmistress Valincia entered the room. "Students, I know you're all very curious about what's happening with the dragons. We teachers are address-ing that now. In the meantime, since this commotion is so disruptive, we're going to suspend classes today so that you may work on Homecoming festivities."

Whinnying and nickering filled the air as the ponies celebrated.

"We're going to have so much fun!" Electra said.

Skydancer felt relieved. Finally, she'd have a chance to contribute to the Earth barn float.

The headmistress whistled to get everyone's attention. "Settle down and listen to your lead ponies. Remember, you're in competition for Grand Pony Marshal. Do your best and follow orders. Maybe you'll be the one proudly wearing that medal!"

Skydancer's smile disappeared. Everyone

was going to hate her when they found out she had lost the medal.

The headmistress continued talking. "We're still not certain what's going to happen with the dragons, but don't worry. We'll take care of it. Enjoy your day off. Where is Skydancer?"

Everyone turned to look at her. "Here," she called out softly.

"The headmaster and I need your assistance. Please come with me."

Skydancer's stomach felt queasy.

"Good luck," Daisy said, as Skydancer headed toward the front of the room. All the ponies were watching. It was so quiet, her clomping hooves seemed louder than ever.

The headmistress led her outside. "I'm sorry to pull you away from the Homecoming preparations, but we can't help the dragons without you and your Glitter Gift."

"That's okay." Skydancer tried not to sound disappointed. She followed the headmistress to the training field where the dragons sat surrounded by the teachers. She was actually happy to see them.

Emerline and Azule smiled at her.

"Skydancer, we need to know what the dragons want us to do," Headmaster Elegius said.

Skydancer nodded. Emerline and Azule looked much more energetic than the day before. Their colors were deeper, too, and their scales were shiny. "How are you feeling today?"

"Much better, thank you so much. I don't know what we'd do without your wonderful translation skills. I wonder if dragons and ponies would've gotten along better years ago if they could've communicated."

"Maybe!" Skydancer said, intrigued by the idea. "Now that you're stronger, what do you want us to do for you?"

"We need to bring some ponies back along with seeds to plant. It would be wonderful to have a huge apple orchard like yours and fields of carrots. But we need quick-growing crops. And we'll need your help planting them and making it rain.

Without pony magic to help things grow, I fear we're doomed."

Skydancer explained this to the teachers.

Headmaster Elegius was quiet for a moment. "Only pegaponies would be able to make the trip—if we decide to go."

"We only have two teachers who are pegaponies," Headmistress Valincia replied.

Professor Xayide was the last remaining flutterpony, no bigger than a hummingbird. Skydancer wondered if he could make the long trip, being so small. And Professor Allandre was a pegapony, but would she want to make the trip all alone? It was a shame Headmaster Elegius couldn't go. He had the most powerful magic of anyone at school.

Then Skydancer had a wonderful idea. "Headmaster, could a pegapony pull the Homecoming chariot in the sky?"

He paused for a moment. "It would have to be a very big and strong pegapony."

"Like Duke?" she asked.

"Send a student with the dragons?" Headmistress Valincia sounded shocked.

Skydancer shivered at the very thought of flying for days to a strange land. She could never do that. She was too scared to dip down into craggy canyon to get the medal back.

"Professor Xayide, can you send for Duke please?" Headmaster Elegius asked.

Professor Xayide sped off into the sky.

"We can provide some food and seeds,

but I don't know that it will be enough for all of them," Headmistress Valincia said.

"I wish we had some more crops to offer," Professor Allandre said.

What else could they send with the dragons? Skydancer wondered. Sugar cubes? Probably not. Those were a rare treat, and there certainly weren't enough to fill up several hungry dragons. Skydancer tried to think of all the wonderful foods she'd enjoyed at school. "I know! We can get seaweed from the seaponies! They have huge fields of it growing underwater. Maybe it could grow where the dragons live."

"That's an excellent idea, Skydancer," the headmaster said.

"Do you think that would work?" Skydancer asked the dragons.

"We do have a large lake, but it's nearly dry," Emerline said.

Skydancer explained the situation to the teachers.

"Well, it's worth harvesting some to bring," Professor Allandre said.

Just then, Professor Xayide returned with Duke. "I explained everything, and Duke would like to come along."

"Duke, it could be a treacherous journey. It will take several days," the headmistress said. "You have to fly over the craggy canyon."

Duke raised his chin to the sky. "Nothing scares me. I'm glad to help."

Skydancer felt embarrassed that she wasn't as brave as Duke was. There weren't that many pegaponies who could make the trip. And it sounded like there was a lot of work to do to help the dragons reclaim their land. They could certainly use her assistance.

"Skydancer, can you ask the seaponies if they'll give us some of their food?" the headmistress asked.

"We need Daisy to help. She's good friends with them."

Someone sent for Daisy, and when she arrived, the group galloped to the river that led to the ocean. Daisy sang a song—music always lures a seapony to the surface.

Sure enough, Marina's shiny head soon bobbed above the water. Her eyes widened when she saw the big crowd gathered. "What's going on?"

Skydancer explained why they needed some seaweed.

"Dragons? Oh my!" Marina said, sliding back underwater.

"But they're nice. They only eat plants now," Daisy called after her.

"We need as much as you can get," Skydancer said.

Marina bobbed back up. "I'll tell everyone below. We'll bring up loads of it before nightfall."

"Thanks!" Skydancer said.

They hurried back to the school. Ponies were crowded outside each barn, working on projects for Homecoming. Skydancer felt sad she couldn't take part in the fun.

"Skydancer, tell the dragons we will leave first thing in the morning," the headmaster said "But our magic isn't as powerful as it once was, and we only have four ponies coming. I'm not sure how successful we'll be."

She told this to Emerline, who nodded sadly. "We appreciate any help you can give us. I have to thank you, Skydancer. I can't imagine anyone would have agreed to help us if you weren't here to share our message."

Skydancer smiled, but despite the kind words, she still didn't feel like she was doing enough. If she were braver, she'd be going on the journey, too.

"I don't know how long we'll be gone," Headmaster Elegius said. "We'll try to return by Homecoming, but I make no guarantees."

Skydancer's ears pricked up. If the headmaster was gone, maybe she could find a way to get the medal back and return it to his office without him knowing it was missing!

CHAPTER 8

Everyone from the school gathered the next morning to bid farewell to the dragons and the ponies going on the journey.

Huge baskets were filled with seaweed, apples, carrots, and seeds for the dragons to carry. A beautiful gold chariot sat on the field, and Headmaster Elegius climbed inside.

"They must be so nervous," Razzle said. "Emerline and Azule are nice, but what about the other dragons? What if they're so hungry they . . ."

Skydancer knew what Razzle was trying to say. She thought the other dragons might eat the ponies. "Don't even say that," Skydancer said. "I'm sure they are just as kind and peaceful."

"Aren't you glad you don't have to go?" Electra asked.

Truthfully, Skydancer was relieved. She didn't want to fly over the craggy canyon. She didn't want to be away from school for days. She was afraid to visit a strange place.

But she was also going to miss the dragons, she realized. And she'd be worried the other ponies wouldn't have enough magic to help the dragons conjure rain for crops.

What if they couldn't help the dragons?

All her fears nipped at her thoughts, but Skydancer did something remarkable anyway. She stepped forward and said, "Headmaster, I volunteer to make the journey. I can fly, and I can communicate with the dragons. I can also help with the weather spells."

A few students gasped. The headmaster nodded thoughtfully. "We certainly could use your help. Are you sure? We don't know what lies ahead."

It meant she wouldn't be able to get the medal back. Or work on the float. She'd be tired from flying and certainly frightened at times. "I'm sure. I want to help."

"Very well," he said. "Thank you." He turned to the rest of the students. "Would any other pegaponies like to join us?"

No one else stepped forward, not even Lavender whose Glitter Gift of making flowers bloom would be incredibly helpful. But Skydancer understood how scared Lavender must be, because she was feeling terrified herself.

"Very well, then. Headmistress Valincia will remain here to look after you all. We will return as soon as we can."

Skydancer's heart was beating so fast. Wait until her parents heard about this! She was their only pony, and they had always been so protective of her, never letting her dash off on adventures with the other ponies in her village. They thought she was too special for such nonsense. Now flying off to help dragons? They'd faint in fright!

But Skydancer lined up with the others ready to take off for the journey. Daisy ran over and nuzzled her nose against her fur. "Be careful. I'm going to miss you."

"I'll miss you, too. Work hard on the float! We have to win."

Daisy promised she would.

They were about to leave for their journey when Skydancer had an idea. "Headmaster, what if all the ponies used our magic together here, before we leave, to enchant the seeds so they grow faster?"

The headmaster nodded. "I'm embarrassed I didn't think of that myself. I'm glad you had the courage to speak up."

Courage? Skydancer thought, surprised. She didn't have courage. None at all.

"Students, teachers, gather round so we can cast a spell upon these seeds," said Headmaster Elegius as he levitated the baskets and set them on the ground. He closed his eyes, moving his lips without making a sound. "I've got the perfect spell!"

"I wonder if this will work?" Daisy asked. "Will the dragons be able to grow enough food?"

"I hope so," Skydancer said.

"Students, teachers, repeat this spell with me," said Headmaster Elegius. "Make each seed . . . grow with speed . . . and quickly become dragon feed."

All the ponies stomped their glittery hooves, charging up their magic. Clouds of sparks billowed. "Make each seed grow with speed and quickly become dragon feed."

The baskets of seeds glistened with magic.

Headmaster Elegius and Professor Xayide climbed into the chariot, while Duke was fastened into the harness.

Skydancer and Professor Allandre would be flying alongside them. Suddenly, she felt terrified. What if she wasn't strong enough to make the journey? What if she got lost again like she had over craggy canyon?

She was so scared, she trembled. But she had to help the dragons. She took a long slurp of water and lined up next to the chariot.

"Good-bye!" called the ponies.

"Good luck!"

Daisy, Razzle, Electra, and Belissima scampered over to Skydancer and nudged noses with her.

"We'll miss you," Electra said.

"Be back in time for Homecoming," Belissima said.

"Be careful!" Razzle warned.

"I'm so proud of you," Daisy said. "Without you, the dragons probably wouldn't survive."

Skydancer felt a lump in her throat. She nodded and blinked back tears, grateful she had such good friends. Then, as Duke galloped and lifted the chariot into the air, and the professors flew off, Skydancer flapped her wings and took flight.

CHAPTER 9

Skydancer shivered as they flew through the cloud bank. And she willed herself not to look down when they flew over the craggy canyon. She was tempted to scan the cliffs for the medal, but was too scared to look.

"We'll be across the canyon shortly," Headmaster Elegius shouted. "Just keep flying. Don't worry."

Skydancer nodded, and soon enough,

they were sailing over lush forests, rivers, and lakes.

The dragons led the way. "We have to fly far away from towns and villages so we don't frighten the humans. Our journey is a little longer that way, but safer," Emerline explained.

By the end of the first day, Skydancer was exhausted. Too tired even to eat food when they landed for the night in a forest grove. She fell right to sleep, dreaming of tumbling medals and roaring dragons.

In the morning, she ate a few carrots and they were off again. She'd never flown so far or for so long. She ached by the time they landed for a break. She flexed her sore wings.

"Are you okay, Skydancer?" asked Headmaster Elegius.

She nodded. "Just tired."

"It was very generous of you to come," he said. "We'll certainly need your help communicating with the other dragons. I'm not sure how they'll react when we arrive."

Skydancer worried about that as they flew on. Would they be angry the ponies were coming to their land? Would they be so hungry that they would try to eat them?

She shook the idea from her mind. The dragons would not hurt them.

As they flew on, she was growing more tired, uncertain she could complete the trip. Even Duke was slowing down. *This was a mistake*, she thought.

Then, just ahead, she saw a huge water-fall streaming out the side of a mountain. Duke headed straight for the rainbow arching in front of it. Skydancer followed. Rainbows temporarily strengthened Glitter Pony magic. She'd experienced it a few times as a young pony when a rainbow would appear after a storm, but she'd never flown through one.

Soon, she was soaring through the intense colors, feeling energized, happy, and excited. She zoomed up into the air shouting, "Yahoo!" They were just one day away from reaching the dragon's world. She had no doubt now she could make it.

They flew faster and longer before settling down for the night. When they woke, Emerline stretched her wings and smiled. "We're just a few hours away now. I can't wait to see my family. They're going to be so relieved we're bringing help."

"How many dragons are there?" Skydancer asked.

"Four families remain. There are eighteen dragons in total."

Not very many dragons, Skydancer thought—but they could still easily overpower the ponies if they wanted to. It was up to Skydancer to quickly communicate with the dragons and let them know they were there to help. She realized being the interpreter for the group was a huge responsibility.

The next day, they flew until the sun was high above them. Emerline called, "It's just ahead, we have to go through a cave that leads to the hidden clearing."

Skydancer had never flown into a cave!

As they approached the mountain, they swooped down and flew into the small opening. It was dark and cramped, so they

landed and walked along until they saw a light ahead.

"We're here," said Emerline.

Azule scampered ahead crying, "Mom! Dad! We're back! We brought the Glitter Ponies with us!"

Skydancer stepped out from the damp tunnel into the bright sun. She looked around in amazement. There was nothing but dirt and rocks on the ground. Tree trunks stood bare, stripped of their leaves and branches.

Then she spotted the giant forms of the dying dragons, almost as dull in color as the dirt. A large one lying near the opening of a cave raised its head and roared.

"Children! What have you done?"

CHAPTER 10

The ponies huddled in a group while Emerline and Azule hurried over to the dragon.

"Remain calm," Headmaster Elegius said.

"I can fight if you need me to," Duke said.

"There will be no fighting today," the headmaster said.

"Dad, we brought help!" Emerline said. "The Glitter Ponies enchanted their seeds to grow quickly, and we brought some seaweed to fill our lake. Bushels of apples and carrots to eat, too."

"How do we know their food is safe?" Emerline's dad asked. "How do we know they're not trying to kill us off for good?"

"Dad, they helped me and Emerline when we went to their school," Azule said. "They're good."

Another dragon groaned. "Ponies can't be trusted. They'll unleash their magic on us."

"Tell them to leave," said another.

"They're our only hope," cried Emerline. "They traveled for days to get here."

Skydancer's heart dropped. How could the dragons think they came here to hurt them?

"What are they saying?" Headmaster Elegius asked.

"They're worried we're going to harm them," Skydancer explained.

The father dragon raised his head. "I can understand you."

Skydancer gulped and walked closer to the huge dragon. "I can speak with winged animals. It's my Glitter Gift. We're here to help. I'm Skydancer. Nice to meet you."

"And I'm Rubrum, father to Emerline and Azule. If you are truly here on a mission of kindness, I fear there's nothing you can do. We're doomed. Nothing grows. The rain doesn't fall."

"Working together, we might be able to make it happen. Just give us a chance," said Skydancer. She returned to the ponies and said, "We should pass out the food and show them we're here to help. Prove we mean no harm."

The three teachers, Duke, and Skydancer passed out apples and carrots to the grateful dragons. A few were reluctant to eat at first, but eventually gobbled up the food. Once they'd eaten, Headmaster Elegius said, "There's no time to waste. We must plant these seeds."

They chose the perfect spot for an orchard and started planting seeds. There were hundreds of them! But they quickly developed a plan: Professor Xayide buzzed across the ground, kicking his back hooves into the dirt, leaving a hole. Then the rest of the ponies dropped the seeds into the divets, swishing their tails over the soil to cover them up.

Skydancer was exhausted and just wanted to rest. But Headmaster Elegius said, "We must join our magic now to make it rain."

Skydancer wasn't sure she could do it, but she gathered with the other ponies in a circle.

"May water from the sky start to fall, so these crops grow for one and all," Headmaster Elegius said.

The ponies started pounding their hooves on the ground, charging their magic. "May water from the sky start to fall, so these crops grow for one and all."

Soon, raindrops were pattering the

ground. They tickled Skydancer's nose. Professor Xayide buzzed through the air shouting, "Hurray!"

Headmaster Elegius nodded and smiled as Duke and Skydancer pranced and trotted beneath the rain.

One by one, the dragons raised their big heads to the sky. The rain washed off the dust and dirt covering their glorious colors. Emerline and Azule stretched their wings and burst into the air, laughing and shrieking as they soared through the showers.

Tiny green shoots unfurled from the dirt, rising toward the sky, until they were small trees dotted with white apple blossoms.

Carrot tops poked through the earth in the fields where they'd been planted.

Skydancer thought her heart might burst, it was such a beautiful scene. She'd done some fun things with her magic: chattered with birds, levitated quills and books. But this was the first time her magic had been used to do something so good.

"Ponies, let's get that lake filled with water," Headmaster Elegius said.

They followed him over to the big lake that now looked like a puddle as the rain started to fall. But it would take more than a few hours of rain to fill it.

"Let me think of the right spell," Headmaster Elegius said.

Skydancer tried thinking of the perfect spell she would use. "What about this, Headmaster? 'With fresh, clean water fill this lake, so there's always plenty for all to take.'"

"That is perfect!"

Again, the ponies charged their magic and repeated the spell. Soon, a cloud appeared over the lake, pouring in water.

The dragons surrounded the lake, cheering.

"Let's get the seaweed in here so it can start growing," said Duke.

They hauled over the baskets and dumped it in.

Rubrum walked over to the ponies. He looked at Skydancer. "I'm sorry we doubted your intentions. How can we ever thank you for saving us?"

Skydancer told the other ponies what he said.

"We're happy to help, and hope this is the beginning of a new friendship. Ponies and dragons shall live in peace from this day forward," Headmaster Elegius said.

Emerline's father nodded when Skydancer repeated the headmaster's words.

"You are welcome to visit anytime," he said.

Skydancer smiled at Emerline and Azule. She certainly would miss them. But she was anxious to get back to school. She didn't want to miss Homecoming. And, maybe, she might be able to solve the problem of the missing medal.

CHAPTER 11

Skydancer was sad to leave the dragons, but happy they'd made a difference. She wasn't worried about the long flight home. Headmaster Elegius promised they could fly through the rainbow again to boost their magic.

"If we stop only for the shortest of breaks, we'll be back in time for the Homecoming celebration," the headmaster said on the second day of flying.

When it was time to cross the craggy canyon, she knew this was her last chance to retrieve the medal. Maybe she could get it back to the headmaster's office before the ceremony.

As they flew across the canyon, she hung back from the group, taking deep breaths to calm herself. She flew toward the tall pine tree that was near the spot she'd dropped the medal.

Once she saw the chariot glide into the cloud bank, she dropped down into the canyon. She hummed to herself so she wouldn't hear the cries of the beasts below. She ignored the goose bumps prickling her hide, trying not to imagine what the creatures looked like. She scanned the side of the canyon, looking at all the branches sticking out—but she didn't see the medal hanging on any of them!

It was lost. The Grand Pony Marshal medal that had been awarded to students for hundreds of years was now gone. Gone forever, and it was her fault.

She caught up to the group and landed near the school entrance. The students cheered and crowded around them.

Daisy galloped over. "I'm so glad you're back home safe. And you're just in time for Homecoming!"

Skydancer nodded. But the last thing she wanted to do was join the festivities. Not with the medal gone.

"I'll meet you there," she told Daisy. "I need to clean up."

But first, she needed to tell Headmaster Elegius what had happened to the medal.

As the students headed for the exhibition field, Skydancer ran up to Headmaster Elegius. "I need to talk to you, Headmaster."

"What is it?"

It took a moment before she could get the words out. "I was supposed to bring the

Grand Pony Marshal medal back to you the day I saw the dragons . . ."

"Yes?"

"And I decided to fly around with it for a while first. And I got distracted and ended up over craggy canyon . . . and dropped it."

Headmaster Elegius said nothing.

"I'm so sorry! I tried looking for it on our way back just now, but it wasn't there."

"You flew into the canyon?" he asked, surprised.

She could only nod.

"Take a moment to clean up and then come to my office."

"Okay." She blinked back tears. Feeling dusty and dirty, she ran back to her stable, conjured a shower to wash off, and headed to the headmaster's office.

"Please come into my office."

With her head hanging low, she walked in, wondering if she was going to be punished or worse. "I'm sorry the medal is lost."

"But it's not," he said.

"Excuse me? I'm confused."

The headmaster walked over to a glass cabinet and opened it. He levitated the medal in the air between them.

"You have another medal?"

"No, that's the same medal. But it's enchanted to return to its home here if it's gone from this perch for more than twelve hours. We've had several Grand Pony

Marshals forget to turn it in right after the ceremony," he said with a wink.

Skydancer blew out a breath. "Thank goodness. I thought I'd ruined everything."

"You're very brave, Skydancer."

Her head snapped up. "What do you mean?"

"You certainly felt very bad about the

medal, but you had the courage to tell me anyway. And you volunteered for a very scary mission."

"But I was scared; I wasn't brave."

"Being brave doesn't mean you're not scared. Being brave means you're scared, but you face your fears and do the scary thing anyway. Without fear, there can be no bravery."

"Wow, I never thought of it that way."

"And I think you'll find your magic has changed after the events of the past week."

"Changed? How?"

"Magic gets stronger when it's used for such great good." He smiled, and Skydancer's heart swelled with happiness. "Now. Let's get over to the ceremony," he said.

Skydancer happily followed the head-master to the exhibition field. She couldn't wait to see the float that Earth barn had created. She'd do her best not to show her disappointment when someone else was named Grand Pony Marshal. But at least the medal wasn't missing! She just hoped her parents weren't too disappointed she wouldn't be wearing it.

CHAPTER 12

The stands were filled with families, and former students with the royal children who had selected them as their pets. Skydancer galloped over to the ponies from Earth barn.

"Wow," Daisy said. "You look so... sparkly."

Skydancer fluttered her wings. She did feel more magical.

"Welcome to the annual Enchanted Pony Academy Homecoming celebration!" said

Headmistress Valincia. "We're so pleased to welcome you back to school. Now, please give a round of applause to this year's Grand Pony Marshal who put in 110 percent effort to work on the float for Sky barn!"

Zander, a second-year unipony from Sky barn, pranced onto the track to great applause. Skydancer felt sad remembering how wonderful it had felt to wear that medal.

Ponies from each barn pulled their floats onto the track around the exhibition field. A rainbow arched over the Sky float. Sun had a mini solar system as its display. Water barn decorated their float so that a waterfall seemed to be falling off the side.

Skydancer and Daisy cheered when Earth barn's float arrived covered in flowers and vines.

The floats were parked in front of the stage, while the teachers finished voting for their favorites.

"We are pleased to announce this year's winner of the float competition!"

Headmistress Valincia said. "Congratulations to Water barn for their impressive display!"

Belissima dropped her head down, and Skydancer felt so bad she hadn't been here to help. But helping the dragons had certainly been more important than working on the float.

Headmaster Elegius quieted the crowd. "I have a very special announcement today. I

would like to present a new award this year given to the two students who have done their best to use their magic for good. Would Duke and Skydancer please come to the podium?"

Skydancer stood frozen until Electra nudged her along. "Go!"

Skydancer flew to the podium as the crowd cheered, joining Duke onstage.

"Congratulations to the first ever winners of our Magic Shining Bright Award." He levitated medals onto each pony's neck.

Headmistress Valincia smiled at them. "Thank you for your special service to the school. May your magic grow and help the world be a better place. You're going to be excellent royal pets someday."

Skydancer couldn't believe it! She saw her parents in the crowd cheering.

As the crowd whinnied and clapped, Skydancer whispered to the headmaster, "I'll be sure to turn the medal in right after the ceremony."

He winked at her. "That's yours to keep. And should it ever get lost, let's say in the craggy canyon, it's enchanted to return to you."

She laughed. "Thank you so much." She flew up into the sky, soaring over the exhibition field, barely believing the beautiful medal was hanging from her chest. She only wished she could show it to Emerline and Azule.

Maybe some day she'd be able to see them again. She was just glad she'd found the courage to become their friend. Now she knew she'd be brave enough to do anything.